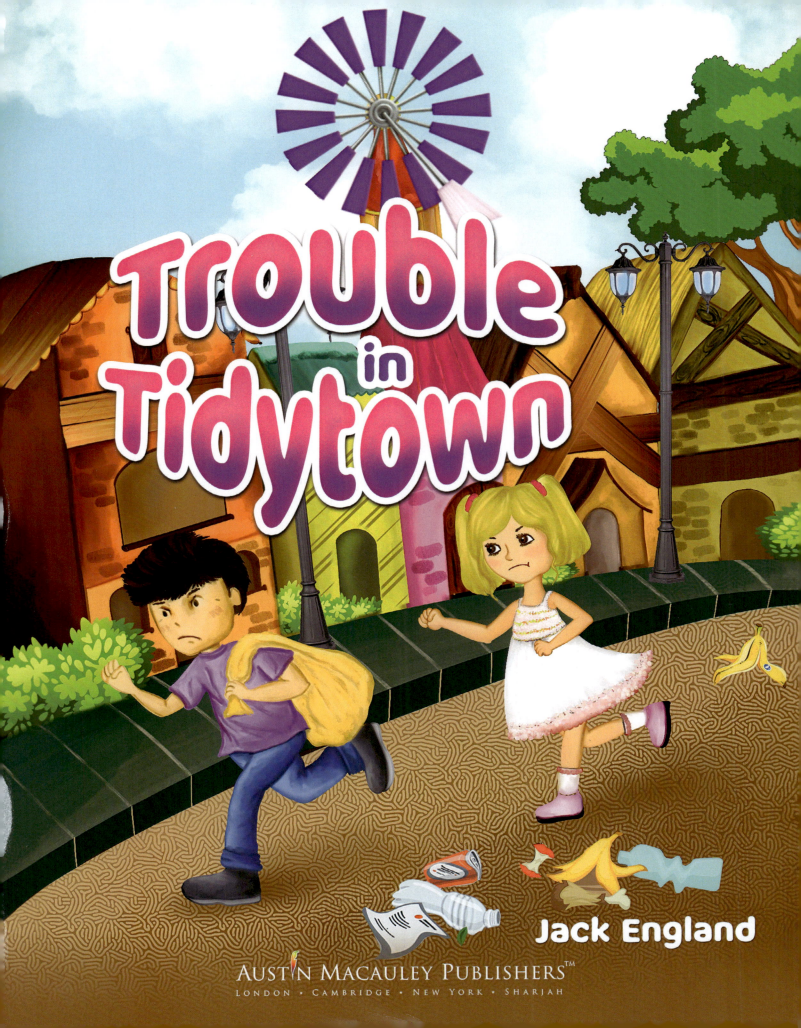

Copyright © Jack England 2022

The right of **Jack England** to be identified as author of this work has been asserted by the author in accordance with sections 77 and 78 of the Copyright, Designs and Patents Act 1988.

All rights reserved. No part of this publication may be reproduced, stored in a retrieval system, or transmitted in any form or by any means, electronic, mechanical, photocopying, recording, or otherwise, without the prior permission of the publishers.

Any person who commits any unauthorised act in relation to this publication may be liable to criminal prosecution and civil claims for damages.

A CIP catalogue record for this title is available from the British Library.

ISBN 9781528988162 (Paperback)
ISBN 9781528988179 (ePub e-book)

www.austinmacauley.com

First Published 2022
Austin Macauley Publishers Ltd®
1 Canada Square
Canary Wharf
London
E14 5AA

For my mum, who taught me not to litter.

# Trouble in Tidytown

Tidytown is a place far, far away,
where fish eat corn and monkeys eat hay,
there are houses and huts of all shapes and sizes,
shops and stores full of surprises.

The roads were clean and the pavements spotless,
Even a king would have walked around
there sockless!
But who do you ask is the leader of this place?

I'll tell you, her name is **Miss Whitelace!**

But **Miss Whitelace**, she had a daughter,
who was just as clean as chlorine water.
Her dresses were neat and her hair even neater,
once she even polished the heater!

"So what is her name?" I know you are wondering,
Sitting and reading this closely and pondering,
Her name is so fair it could befit a queen,
For her name is **Catherine** and she's ever
so clean.

**Clean Catherine** wandered on cobble and cement,
Her mind full of happiness, not a single lament.
She looked all around, everything was gleaming,
She saw something foul and thought she was dreaming.

**Dirty Dexter**, the villain of this town,
Who always walked round with such a big frown,
Had thrown, so carelessly, a red soda can,
Onto the floor in his dastardly plan.

He ran to the farm, where old man **Michael**
Worked all day as the windmill cycled.

**Dexter** didn't care, he just wanted to spoil,
The beautiful town and the delicate soil.

Old man **Michael**, he was very upset,
Looking at the rubbish he threw out a threat,

"I'll get you **Dexter**, you won't get away,
With all that you've done, you've ruined my hay!"

**Dirty Dexter** continued to run,
Throwing around litter was ever so fun!
He tossed and he flung, he lobbed and hurled,
All of the rubbish in the entire world.

**Catherine** however, was close behind,
Chasing him down and keeping in mind,
To clear all the litter that had been thrown down,
As the people of Tidytown were beginning
to frown.

**Susie Swan** was tangled in plastic,
She struggled and wriggled, the situation drastic.
**Henry Hedgehog** had gotten his head stuck,
Inside of a tin can covered in black muck.

She carried on going, helping the folk,
That **Dirty Dexter** proceeded to provoke.
She ran on quickly staying near,
Close to him now; he called out sneer,

"You'll never catch me, I'll never be caught,
You may be sad, you may be distraught,
But you see young child of this small town,
You might be mad, but I'll never back down!"

**Clean Catherine** pulled back, looking ahead,
Her face suddenly flooded with dread,
"Watch out **Dexter**! You're going too fast!
Keep going like that and you'll be in a cast!"

But **Dirty Dexter** kept on running,
Throwing out rubbish, he was ever so cunning,
He never noticed, he didn't feel,
That he had just slipped on a banana peel!

**Dirty Dexter** hit the ground,
Seeing the mistake of his terrible round,
He looked at the floor and then at the trash,
Only just noticing the hideous gash.

His knee was injured and his feelings hurt,
The damage he'd done was clearly overt.
He pulled himself up and walked to the child,
Knowing his littering had made her so riled.

**Clean Catherine** looked up and smiled softly,
She knew he regretted being so brawly,
"Come on **Dexter,** let's clean this up,
Right over there, we'll start with that muck."

**Catherine** and **Dexter** walked all around,
Picking the rubbish up from the ground,
They collected and gathered, put it all in,
A great, big bag and into the bin.

They looked all around,
everything was spotless,
Even a king would have walked around
there sockless,

**Dexter** and **Catherine** they turned to
each other,
They were pleased with their work and
called to her mother,

**Miss Whitelace**, she came out of the
house in a hurry,
Her face was all red like she'd eaten a curry!
She smiled and she beamed, she was pleased,
To see the day her daughter had seized.

And **Dirty Dexter**, you're asking what happened,
To him and his plan to make the world saddened.
He'd changed his ways and now you will see,
That **Dexter's** just as clean as can be!